10 Deadly Aspects of Pride

10 Deadly
Aspects of
PRIDE

By:

Dr. Eric L. Johnson

BookVenture Publishing LLC
1000 Country Lane Ste 300
Ishpeming MI 49849
www.bookventure.com
Hotline: 1(877) 276-9751
Fax: 1(877) 864-1686

Ordering Information:
Quantity sales. Special discounts are available on quantity purchases by corporations, associations, and others. For details, contact the publisher at the address above.

Printed in the United States of America.

Library of Congress Control Number:		2016935261
ISBN-13:	Paperback	978-1-944849-26-9
	Pdf	978-1-944849-27-6
	ePub	978-1-944849-28-3
	Kindle	978-1-944849-29-0

Rev. date: 06/03/2016

CONTENTS

DEDICATION

The first is my uncle Ronald E. Palmer, a man whose relationship with pride was wrought with many of the complexities identified in this book. His relationship with pride contributed to his sense of love, commitment, and his relationships with his loved ones. None among us can live this life without bad decisions, mistakes and unutilized wisdom. His journey was not the exception, however those he loved were aware of that love no matter how complicated it may have been. I have a profound persistent sadness that his bellow of a laugh will never come across my ears again. That heavy reality is mediated by the fact that the lessons he taught me continue to aid me in my own complicated journey. Uncle Ronnie, as I called him, was more than an uncle to me. He was as much a father figure to me as any other man in my life.

The second is my grandmother Cora Caver, a beautiful kind woman whose relationship with pride was not absent many of the challenges addressed in this book. Nonetheless, her importance in my life cannot be overstated. It was she who first demonstrated the meaning compassion and love in a way that even a child could understand. My grandmother left a whole in my life that could never be filled. I take comfort in that I leave these words to mark her impact on my life to stand long after I join her on the next part of the journey.

Pride is a complicated concept replete with a myriad of potential challenges and quagmires that make its presence at best, convoluted. The pleasure that pride offers is intoxicatingly euphoric in that it feeds the most basic components of the human ego. Each of us understandably wants to feel good about the things we or the people we care about accomplish or achieve. A joy that emanates from success despite adversity is one well deserved and appropriate. However, joy has a tendency to appreciate all the contributing factors that function outside conscious control. Moreover, joy tends to have an appreciation for all the dynamics that could have been detractions that were not for no rational reason. Lastly, joy often accounts for the faith and humility that are required to appreciate the two earlier points.

Conversely, pride tends to be an inward celebration by the ego that at best, dismisses essential supportive structures and at worst, denies their existence altogether. Pride often invites one to oversimplify desired occurrences as the result of conscious will with little attention to an uncontrolled environment. Indeed, the pleasure offered by pride is analogous to drinking salt water; the more you drink, the more you need. A cycle that ends with only one result, the death of the drinker. This book attempts to identify the ubiquitous presence pride tends to have in our lives and the challenges that results from it. Moreover, this book advances the notion that pride functions as a primary contributor to much of the mental, spiritual and emotional instability present in our society. To the extent that we contain pride, we release the potential of imagination and fulfillment offered by peace and joy.

INTRODUCTION

Pride as a concept is very misunderstood by many who claim that is has redeeming qualities when indeed it has few, if any at all. Pride in this work refers to an overestimation of the abilities, knowledge or importance of an individual, family, institution and sometimes a nation. The overestimation referred to here can be centered in one, two or all three factors and in any combination. The overestimation identified in this definition allows for an unwilling and sometimes, willing blindness to the boundaries of any single actor limited by human capacity.

It is important to make the distinction between pride and several relevant concepts that include Self-respect, self-confidence and faith. Self-respect is an idea that refers to a worth that one has for oneself. The appraisal of that worth can be appropriate, over-estimated or underestimated. Pride is a descriptor of the worth one can have for oneself but it is not a synonym for the concept of self-respect. Meaning, one can have a positive sense of self image and demonstrate behaviors consistent with having a positive sense of self but having a positive sense of self is not synonymous with pride. A positive sense of self allows one to perceive their beliefs and behaviors to be in congruence. Believing that one operates in consistency in terms of behavior and beliefs is not necessarily pride. Pride tends to be a factor when one overestimates what the congruence means. To the extent that one overestimates their importance and relevance because of their perceived congruence is the extent to which a positive sense of self can become prideful. Self-confidence refers to the idea that one believes that given the appropriate effort, resources and circumstances, something can be achieved. Pride would be distinguished from self-confidence in that it suggests the ability to achieve something no matter what circumstances were presented. A reality that can almost never be true. Faith is the belief that for no rational reason, one has an expectation for an event to occur or not occur but the belief is not subject to any limitations grounded in human control. Meaning, one can believe something is going to happen or not happen but not know how or why. In that instance, pride is not an appropriate descriptor because the actor is not the source of the explanation. Pride as a concept makes the relevant individual or individuals the source of the explanation. Whenever the individual or individuals are not the source, pride as a concept is less relevant, if it is relevant at all.

Many who claim that pride has redeeming qualities are those who have succumbed to the pseudo-benefits it uses to suborn acquiescence. Positive notions of pride provide its subscribers with the necessary images to justify their perceived existence. In the pages to come, the reader will be invited to explore the impact of pride in the 10 identified areas but the reader should be encouraged to guard against pride in any context he or she feels compelled to do so.

Chapter I

PRIDE, A SPIRITUAL ENEMY

"The dangers that pride presents to spirituality make it a formidable foe."

Spirituality?

Defining the concept of spirituality is no small matter.
Spirituality is a contested term and an idea with more subjectivity
than most would be willing to admit. The deeply subjective nature
of spirituality renders a series of complexities that have nothing
specifically to do with pride. For many people, the notions
spirituality and religion are deeply connected and in some ways
inseparable, while for others, there is a clear demarcation that
separates the two ideas. In many spiritual understandings, there
is a centralized omnipotent being/energy and others choose to
identify principles and ideas as the grounding force. An exact
definition of spirituality is at best problematic and at worst, it is a
notion that is violently contentious. In the face of deep subjectivity
and adamant disagreement, there are some fundamental
elements that tend to be present in many concepts of spirituality.
There is a tendency for spiritual understandings to include an
awareness that extends beyond the perspective of an individual
life. Meaning, one is often invited to consider circumstances and
implications greater than one's own needs and wants. Moreover,
spiritual explanations often encourage a consideration of the self
in the context of greater circumstance and implication for the
purpose of growth and/or transformation.

Spiritual perspectives routinely summon a compelling
desire to investigate the meaning of life with more emphasis
on the investigation than on a particular outcome. While there
is no consensus on the definition of spirituality, most involve
a sense of humility that encourages the submission of our
worldly needs to something we believe to be more significant. A
submission to something more important than ourselves seems
to be a fundamental component of most ideas purported to be
grounded in spiritual understandings. While the reason, method
and purpose of spiritual submission invariably vacillate with each
understanding, investigating the importance of an individual's

earthly sojourn persists as a pillar in many spiritual frameworks. The element of deference often found in the myriad of spiritual viewpoints has at best, a complicated relationship with notions of pride.

Why is Pride a Spiritual Enemy?

Pride is not a spiritual enemy because it can invite a self-respect often associated with doing what a person believes is right. Certainly, some understandings of pride have the potential to be instrumental in developing the fortitude to stand with right and unpopular principles during trying times. Moreover, one can make the argument that pride is a necessary factor to speak truth to power, especially when done at one's own risk, physical or otherwise. Indeed, some form of pride can be useful as a mechanism for self-development. All things considered, one could make the argument that there are elements of pride that can be perceived as both positive and essential. The question still remains, why is pride a spiritual enemy?

While certainly, pride as a principle has the tendency to help us find worth in ourselves and the fruits of our labor. Spirituality encourages us to find worth in almost everything else. To the extent that we find meaning in the world we inhabit, the better we are able to understand any value we add to it. The value we add to our world often serves as a source for our pride in one way or another. However, when our individual value is not calculated and contextualized within the framework of our purpose for being, then one is confronted with the question: What purpose does our pride serve?

In the absence of relating our prideful moments to our purpose, we experience a sense of pleasure not rooted in any meaningful growth experience. When we experience pride in the absence of a growth experience, it is the equivalent of eating a meal replete with empty calories that is appealing to our sense of taste. If done infrequently, no harm done. To the contrary, a sense of self that is built on prideful moments, absent meaningful growth experiences and consideration of one's purpose, bloats our appreciation of our own value. To the extent that one is tempted to perceive our prideful accomplishments without all the sacrifice that others have made to bring them into reality, contradicts our very existence. Not one of us breathing brought ourselves into existence and anything we accomplish is subservient to that fact alone. How many of us fed ourselves as children? How many of us served as our first teachers? What accomplished person stands as such with a first opportunity they gave to themselves? How many of us operate in the world without any use of the wisdom of those who came before us? These and many other questions are important for consideration as we stuff ourselves with prideful images, thoughts and attitudes. That social, spiritual and psychological diet is not that unlike a food diet replete with empty calories. It is possible to live on such a diet with serious health consequences and as such, our identity can live on such a diet with far more grave consequences.

In an endeavor such as life things that are complicated and we don't know far more than we do know. In a world where what we don't know dwarfs what we do know in comparison, the role of pride is tenuous at best. If an enemy is something that serves as an adversary, foe or threat, pride is a spiritual enemy simply for the threats it poses to our spiritual identity. Each of us has to navigate and respond to those threats on our own terms but it starts with the understanding that there is a danger in pride that we would all be wise to consider.

How does that Affect Other Aspects of Life?

The impact that pride can have on all areas of life can be quite profound. It is important to note that each of us will assess the effect of pride on our lives in our own way. It may be more appropriate to base this approach on a series of questions that each of us will have to answer for ourselves. How does pride affect what I see in the mirror? How has pride complicated my relationships? What role does pride play in my professional ambition? How does pride relate to my desire to be more? The answers to the questions posed here require both a self-reflection and a spiritual development that is neither painless nor common.

In the absence of spiritual consideration, pride has the power and influence to oblige our mirrors to do its bidding. Prideful glazes or glances in the mirror have the ability to display all the things we wish were but are not, while simultaneously hiding in plain sight all the things we choose not to see. In essence, looking into a mirror is as much a spiritual performance as going to a place of worship. In either case, we will take from it what we need. What we take from our mirrors will invariably be reflected in every relationship in which we are connected. In the mirror, do we see a kind person who seeks only to be loved? Do we see a person who offers their flaws as strengths? Do we see a person with the desire to be more and invites what is necessary to make it so?

Whatever the mirror illustrates for us serves as the offering we make to every potential relationship. The role pride plays in the construction of the image in the mirror is the same role it plays in the performance of its representative. Meaning, however we give meaning to the image we perceive in the mirror not only informs what we see but also drives our behavior when we leave it. While there are those who may underestimate the impact of pride on our mirror's representative, that in no way is permission to abdicate our obligation as the director of the performance. Our mirror's representative's performance in the world often times functions as our professional aspiration, getting its authority from our spiritual audacity.

Meaning, if we believe we have a purpose that belongs solely to us, and then our journey is to travel a road that connects where we are to where we need to be. If we are inattentive to our purpose, pride endangers us to believe that we are already what we need to be thereby losing the opportunity to be more. More importantly, stealing the prospect of learning what we need to achieve that for which we were purposed. The dangers that pride presents to spirituality make it a formidable foe. Its greatest asset is our tendency to underestimate its threat to what we claim we want on our journey.

Chapter II

PRIDE, A CHIEF SUPPORTER OF ENVY

"The dark and decadently ruthless nature
of this intersection has the potential
To realize the worst of humanity."

The Impact of Envy in our Lives

Envy much like pride, is a complicated emotion that presents a host of challenges in our lives that warrant attention. It is not unreasonable to assume that many aspirations in life are rooted in the realities revealed to us both as children and adults. In fact, many of the goals we set for ourselves are based on the ideas, images and circumstances to which we have been exposed. It is difficult to imagine the achievement of goals for which we have no frame of reference but indeed, that often does happen. So when does using the success of others to develop goals for ourselves spasm into envy?

This indeed is a significant question that priests, pastors, philosophers and societies have been struggling with for thousands of years. Much of our material accumulation or our individual accomplishments can be rooted in our desire to acquire possessions and achieve goals we have seen in others. It may be appropriate at this point to distinguish jealousy and envy. In most cases, jealousy refers to a fear of losing or having lost the affection of someone to another. Envy on the other hand, is the resentment of someone else's possessions, quality of being or achievements. One can wish they had them or that another did not. Envy is not limited simply to the coveting of material things. Unfortunately, we can envy other people's happiness, intelligence and even someone's joy. While for the most part envy targets things other people have that we crave, but its origin lies in the internal insecurity we have about our own existence.

We don't just envy the good things about others or the materials they possess, we covet those things because of our own spiritual malnourishment. When we envy, we do it at least in part because we believe if we possessed the things we desire, we could escalate our own value. The more time we spend envying the external possessions of others, the less time we spend cultivating and cherishing the phenomena in our own spirit that makes each of us worthy of the life force we enjoy. Envy encourages us to dismiss the fact that each of us brings something into creation that without our spirit would not be. Sometimes, even when our spirit is resilient enough to remind us of our gifts, envy can persuade us that our gifts are less important. The moment we give in to envy, it begins a spiritual spiral that leads one to despair, disillusion and disheartenment.

The strain this spiral can exact on even our closest relationships can do irreparable damage and this includes the relationship we have with ourselves. The state of envy in our society is alarming. If it was not, why would so many be working so hard to be something other than them? Envy presents significant challenges to our spirit on its own merit. Where envy meets pride is a place that not only is disillusioned and sad but it justifies its right to be so with the will and validation to injure others.

How does Pride Support Envy?

The support that pride affords envy is both dark and decadently ruthless. Each of these characteristics apart is significant challenges to personal development. Complicatedly in addition, each presents at least a modicum of potential positivity in our daily lives. However, when these two emotions join forces in a single heart and head, the potential damage in some ways is unimaginable, at least in their extreme expressions. What happens when someone or some people covet something that other people have and they feel they have the right and will to have it for themselves?

As envy preys on our insecurities advanced by the desire to be loved and valued, pride attempts to resolve the tension with a rationalization that justifies why we should have what we yearn for but not why we should earn it. When we envy the possession of material items, pride gives permission to acquire them by any means necessary. However, when we envy non-material things such as joy, happiness or love, pride turns its attention to not why we should have them but why someone else should not. As a result, pride supports envy to resolve the anxiety by utilizing the available means to remove it from the target. A process driven by the question: How can one's joy, happiness or love be removed? The answers to such questions foster an environment that is toxic to all its inhabitants, not just the target.

Indeed, when left unchecked, this motivation can become a purpose unto itself, planting chaos and disorder at every opportunity. Pride becomes a carbon-dioxide that feeds the trees of self-doubt that gives birth to the potential envy that resides within most of us. On the contrary, this dynamic is not limited to individual behavioral interactions. This behavioral modus operandi has tempted and tempts families, groups and even nations. Many a war and genocidal events have their roots at the intersection of pride and envy. The dark and decadently ruthless nature of this intersection has the potential to realize the worst of humanity. A return from this place is not uncomplicated and is riddled with a wake of deceit, betrayal and destruction. Our best defense from such a state is to never go there in the first place. Unfortunately, the world is populated with a voluminous number of people and groups who reside there.

When we occupy space where these people are present, our options are limited. We have an incessant duty to shine our light at all times but we would be prudent to operate with caution when in company with such people. To be sure, these people are not invisible because the space is dark but they are motivated to shun the light. If we are the shining light, they are motivated to be elsewhere. Our obligation to our loved ones who find this intersection is to feed their soul with the value they bring to the world but only they can develop a map that connects where they are to where they need to be. There are many routes that can lead us to the juncture of pride and envy and consequently, it is important to confront our own vulnerabilities and their impact on our lives with some regularity. We should embrace questions such as: What do I fear? What does my fear motivate me to do? How do I engage in my own spiritual protection?

How might Pride and Envy Impact our Ideas?

The most common and less true points of entry to this question is to suggest that we are absent of both pride and envy. It is true that each of us brings something into creation that otherwise would not be, but it is also true that each of us is always in a place that exists between where we are and where we are going. In that state of existence, we are always less than what we could be. It is a constant state of development in the best case scenario and/ or a state being completely absent growth in the worst. Each of us appreciates something about the world that we want but do not have. That appreciation includes characteristics, objects, qualities, professional aspirations and much more. Serious questions come to bear when we want things we don't have, when we are pursuing qualities we don't yet embody and when our eyes covet possessions in the world that we don't need. In some ways, pride sustains the belief that given the time, work and effort, we can have our wants and needs fulfilled.

However, the complexity is that we live in a world with some flaws that we will leave here with. How much effort are we willing to offer to the unknown? What corners are we willing cut to shorten our perceived journey? How much do we believe in our own purpose? These questions help us understand our personal relationship with pride and envy because each of us is as much impacted by our weaknesses as we are by our strengths. That reality provides the opening for envy to flourish. If we do not confront the role that our fears and weaknesses play in our lives, we provide pride and envy with an invitation to wreak havoc. There is no particular dishonor in the awareness that we are not the embodiment of what we believe we ought to be. Nor is there any particular shame to want possessions that we see in the custody of those in our eyesight. However, in the same way that seeds are planted in the dirt to grow trees, desire is a seed that is planted in our hearts with the potential to develop into envy.

There are none among us who are absent of desire in the myriad of ways that desire expresses itself in the human experience. Desire in its seed form provides a healthy call to action or the motivation to achieve what we want. However, when that seed grows into the tree of envy with its malignant branches of resentment and pride, our spirits are threatened in its expression. It may be spiritually judicious for each of us to habitually take stock of that which we desire and its influence on our decision making. Not doing so can be hazardous to our personal development and our spiritual health. There certainly is no single answer that speaks to everyone but there is a jeopardy that applies to anyone. "How might pride and envy impact our ideas?" is a question that each of us has to answer for ourselves but it is almost never appropriate to dismiss the question out of hand. As we maneuver to obtain longed for possessions or develop plans to achieve goals and objectives, it is never reckless to occasionally account for the role desire (a precursor to envy) plays in what we value as a possession.

Is it Possible to Envy and Love Simultaneously?

Envy and Love have connections that may not be readily apparent to an uncritical investigation. While envy is a coveting of characteristics and/or possessions because of some value they represent in our world, Love is at least in part, a desire to be valued and/or a value we have assigned to someone or something. Often, when we conceptualize love, it simultaneously suggests some value we believe we have and it also constructs a sense of worth to something or someone in our conscious world. The product of this perceived worth is in part something that we covet. While certainly this is not meant to intimate that the presence of coveting and desire necessarily denotes the presence of envy, but where there is desire, envy has a tendency to seek an audience.

Love is a desire that we covet with such intensity that for its presence, sometimes we are willing to lie, cheat, destroy, steal, compromise, settle or even murder. Each of these are familiar actors in any theatre that stars envy. While there are those who would argue that true love invites the presence of justice, mercy, joy, honesty, growth, aspiration and peace, unfortunately, the sobering reality is that love can and does invoke both. The persistent incursion of envy into any individual life is enduring and it is for that reason that a vigilant investigation of our hearts and spirits is not simply a recommendation but a painful spiritual exam that we must perform with some regularity. We have to honestly and critically ask ourselves several important questions. Who do we love? Why do we love them or it? How are our fears expressed in that love? What does the love invite me to do? Does my understanding of this love invite me to own the challenges it represents? These questions and others are profoundly relevant as we attempt to navigate a very interestingly uncertain aspect of our identity.

Can we love and envy simultaneously? At first glance, this question compels some very obvious responses but upon further reconnaissance, most of us are probably less confident than we were at its initial divulging. How much of our love can be attributed to envy may be a disturbing proposition for some? At the very least, most initial occasions to love are probably presented with some unconscious and unintentional confrontation with some clandestine bout we are having with envy. While the nexus between love and envy is more nebulous than most are willing to confess or even understand, the presence of both love and envy concurrently, undoubtedly insinuates an identity crisis that warrants consideration. The answer to the question would probably vary based upon who is responding. How would you answer the question?

Chapter III

PRIDE, AN ARCH ENEMY OF LOVE

*"Love is our connection to things
we believe give our life meaning."*

How is Pride the Arch Enemy of Love?

Love is a complicated topic that for some, conjures notions of their worth, sacrifice, commitment and a deep sense of meaning, and for the others, love summons notions of disappointment, betrayal, abandonment and pain. Problematically in most, the notion of love petitions all the above. There is no shortage of definitions of the term love. If one is interested in this author's conceptualized notion of love, please reference a previous work *Beyond Self Help*. Otherwise, feel free to consult a source you determine to be valid. Love means many different things to many different people including: What it is? How it should function? What are its requirements? How people should operate within it? And a host of other issues not specifically identified here.

In this approach, it is the preference of the author that the reader determine that for herself or himself, if love is in part a desire to be in connection with a person, an idea, your Creator, your family or whatever you choose to love. We have to in part define what that connection means to us. Meaning, we have to answer all the questions posed earlier and others we may have. Are we the sole source of determination for the perimeters and operation of the loves for which we are connected? How do we account for the limitation of our understandings in our love? What role does forgiveness play? At any given time, how aware are we of our flaws and their impact? These are not insignificant dynamics in love relationships. Pride is significant because more often than it should, pride can suggest to us that we have answers that we indeed do not. Pride helps to establish within us a sense of worth that in part adds to our value. However, when left unchecked, pride cancerously infects our ability to see past our individual desires, wishes, imperfections and weaknesses. The result often leads to less of a connection than was the originally intended. If love at its most elemental component is a desire, then the challenge that pride presents is that it blinds us to our contribution to lessening that connection.

Pride serves as an arch enemy to love in that it is a direct threat to the connections we desire to have on whatever terms we use to define it. Love is our connection to things we believe give our life meaning. As we learn, grow and live, the meanings of these connections undergo shifts, changes, challenges and metamorphoses that either reinforces those connections or they serve as lubricators that loosen the connection. If that is not the desired result, then care has to be taken to contain prideful pursuits that meet our individual desires at the expense of the connections we have determined to be meaningful. In other words, pride can disconnect you in places that you wish to be connected. Love is certainly an idea and emotion that has profound impact on the lived experience of any individual.

It is the legacy of connections and disconnections that serve as noteworthy footnotes of our life story. If one wishes to assess the significance of one's presence, she or he need only examine: What connections do I hold dear? Why are those connections important to me? Who have I disconnected from that I regret? What about me make disconnection a worthy option? What ideas am I connected to that disconnect me from people I care about? These questions and others like them are not frivolous as we seek to contain our own prideful pursuits that threaten to disconnect us from places we in fact wish to be deeply connected. Pride is the arch enemy of love because it has the power to convince us that our individual pursuits are more important than the connections that help feed our soul, give our life meaning and support us during times of crisis. If only pride could dry tears, lift a heavy heart, give a supporting hug or bring the joy offered by the presence of grace and mercy. It would be far more effective to forge connections and promote growth. The impact of pride on our relationships can be more destructive on us than on the people with which we share space.

29

What are the Dangers for me and the People I Claim to Love?

Pride offers many dangers to us and the people we claim to love. First and foremost, pride encourages jeopardies related to complacency. When complacency is present, it lures us to be less aware of the work that love often requires. The work related to love has to do with growth, inspiration and support. The effort to both receive and transmit these elements in most, if not all our love relationships, is steady to say the least. To consistently project those elements to the people we claim to care about requires an attentive awareness to our world that is often at odds with most attitudes associated with complacency.

If complacency is in part a security that is present because of unperceived potential dangers, then is it possible that our prideful interests can present unwarranted security and hide potential hazards? Our love connections are important mechanisms by which we measure our sense of meaning to our world. In almost any meaningful way we can construct, that would include the extent to which we invite growth, inspiration and support in the people we love and how they do the same for us. Pride challenges that meaningful goal because it gives us permission to not make that a priority. Pride provides the mind, spirit and heart with reasons to give precedence to other more worldly needs deemed to be in our best interest. When left unchecked, pride encourages us to become relationship mercenaries; people who seek the fulfillment of their own needs with little conscious attention to anything else.

In that mode of operation, the needs of others are considered only as they relate to the goals of the mercenary. Pride provides relationship mercenaries with all the justification necessary to give as little as possible and to take as much as imaginable. Certainly, mercenaries are extreme expressions in relationship paradigms but the moment we stop accounting for complacency, we submit an application to mercenary university and there is an accelerated program where the degree is conferred in very short periods of time. While certainly there a host of dangers that pride poses to the people we care about but it also takes a toll on the "self" as well. Pride lessens our individual awareness of the areas we are in need of growth, inspiration and support. Consequently, we are then without the very tools we need to become whatever it is we have claimed we want to be. This is further complicated by the fact that without those tools, we don't have a device to assess neither the damage nor the rebuilding process. In this state of mind, pride uses the self as its sole source of nourishment and attempts to feed and consume simultaneously, a process that is not ideal under any circumstances. The dangers that pride tenders to us and the people we claim to love are serious. There are those who would snub pride's role in disconnecting us in places that we wish to be connected, or who would furthermore discount the role of pride in our distorted personal development, but doing so is akin to standing in the hole with the shovel.

What are Important Ideas to Consider Going Forward?

The relationship between love and pride is complicated at best and at worst, they are the antithesis of one another. If pride is in part finding value in ourselves and love helps us find value in ourselves and others, then there are probably some important ideas we should explore as we apply these terms both separately and collectively. Collectively, these ideas find relevancy in our insecurities and vulnerabilities. Love is in part a mechanism that allows us to constructively fill the holes created by our anxieties and self-doubt. It does so by providing us the opportunity to share in the successes of others while simultaneously learning from their mistakes.

Furthermore, love allows us to utilize the vision and perspectives of others to navigate jagged, dangerous and uncertain obstacles that have the potential to inflict unsmiling harm on our lives. While love attempts to respond to our insecurities with long term sustainable resolutions, pride approaches this task with more shortsighted methods. Pride does not seek long terms resolutions to uncertainties. Quite to the contrary, pride tends to favor quick responses that are frequently superficial in nature. Rather than using the wisdom of others to engage in a process that encourages growth in our spirit, pride attempts to patch the holes left by our insecurities with materials that amount to little more than wet paper towels. The spotty and unreliable work that pride does in its response to our liabilities and susceptibilities often results in proliferation rather than sustainable resolution. When considered separately, these notions are surprisingly multifarious.

Many of the complexities of pride have already been addressed and there are many more to come but as it relates to love, pride often supports what provides pleasure rather than what is healthy when the two are not the same. Pride tends to rationalize the compromise of love rather than inspire its integrity. Pride tends to opt for short term gratification when love calls for long term investigation. If we seek to deepen our connections to the people we love, it would behoove us all to be aware of the extent to which our life circumstances are informed by short terms desires or sustainable long term resolutions. While the two are clearly discernable in the light of sober deliberation, pleasure seeking enterprises can be compellingly powerful motivations that give permission to be less vigilant in our decision making than we otherwise might be. Pride and love are notions housed in the subconscious human desire to find value in our own existence. Their persistence in the human experience helps to fuel the motivation to measure the meaning of our worth. It is probably more advantageous that we reconcile our individual orientation to the connection of these two ideas in our lives than it is to assume our current positioning with these ideas warrants no further analysis.

Chapter IV

PRIDE, A SOCIAL DEGENERATE

"Oftentimes individual growth and collective success require an appreciation for areas in need of development that prideful lenses tend to hide."

How does Social Understanding Contribute to the Human Experience?

Human social groups occur for a myriad of reasons. Fundamental to all social groups, from couples and friendships to communities and nations, is the idea that each individual is better served by participating in a group. The survival of the group often rests on each individual submitting to the success of the group and thereby supporting their own interest. The implicit social contract of any group is the basic idea that promoting the group's interest furthers the interest of all its members. The success of any social assembly rests on the extent to which this contract is honored by all concerned parties. Humans use social connections as a mechanism to live beyond the perimeter of each of our individual boundaries.

When operating as a collective, cooperatively pooling our resources, we frequently discover and exceed the boundaries of our understanding. However, this boundless potential is realized at a price. The survival of the group must take precedence over individual pursuits when there are irreconcilable differences. In this paradigm, each individual is less important than the collective but not less important than any other single individual. One has to be clear here. This is not intended to be an introduction to communism or socialism. Each idea expressed thus far are relevant in any social collective where humans co-habitat as a society. Societies require the sacrifice of its members on occasion for the maintenance of their existence. This is true of any relationship, marriage, family, community or nation.

Pride complicates these arrangements because it can invite some to assign value in ways that knock the collective off balance. This imbalance is expressed in a number of ways. Part of the collective begins to operate with less consideration for the group and more for their own interests. They do so because they believe they know better, because they believe important principles have been violated or because they believe they are obliged to right an apparent wrong. What was a collective endeavor becomes a competition of the survival of the fittest where there are no winners. If the collective afforded opportunities to individuals that otherwise would not exist, then those opportunities are less realized in the absence of the collective.

Dynamic discussions about the survival of the collective and each member's responsibility to contribute disfigure into frequent prospects to denunciate, accuse and criticize, with little concern for reconciliation and resolution. Members are forced to either realize those opportunities for themselves or they are driven to participate in another collective. Pride is an important element because when tensions are high and answers are scarce, it can suggest that winning the fight and being right is synonymous with protecting the interests of the collective. In circumstances such as those, all parties claim the high ground when in all actuality there was none to be taken. It is always important to distinguish finding joy in the existence of the collective is not the same as being prideful about one's contribution to it. In this way, pride becomes a social degenerate that either makes the collective less than what it could be or in worst case scenarios, dissolves the collective altogether.

What is Degenerate about Pride?

If degenerate is an inclination to become less complex or a process to become mathematically simpler, how does that relate to pride? While pride has a tendency to invite one to assess the value or contribution of someone or something, it does little to identify our natural human shortcomings to ourselves. Oftentimes, individual growth and collective success require an appreciation for areas in need of development that prideful lenses tend to hide. In addition, social collectives are often predicated on the balance of individual importance and collective aspiration.

Where individual inadequacies intersect with collective hope and desire is a place where most societies find meaning and legitimacy. Societies and all social collectives are most relevant at that juncture where individual capacity is expanded by a sense of shared responsibility. All social collectives rely on its member's awareness of shared interdependence. Pride is degenerate because of its tendency to coalesce around an individual's importance and benefaction. Social degenerates allow pride to not only inform their behavior but it tends to heavily impact the prism by which one understands the function of broader society. Rather than understand the purpose of something and its function in society, pride invites one to assess societal functions and roles through the spectrum of self-interest.

As a consequence, pride gives permission to assign more value to the things determined to be in one's self interest with less regard to its purpose for the collective. In this perspective, individual behavior is less concerning than the institutional corruption that can become the ultimate result. Social degenerates are not simple individuals with distorted senses of individual value and entitlement, but they are also organizations and institutions that employ policies and procedures that ultimately call into question their legitimacy. Organizations and institutions are the chief mechanisms by which collectives share resources, identify important challenges, institute societal responses and maintain order. It is not possible to execute and achieve any of those goals without mistakes and grievances. It is however essential that members of a collective believe that institutions and organizations are operating in the interest of collective aspiration even when it is not in the interest of individual desire.

When institutions and organizations allow pride to disproportionately impact organizational procedure by allowing organizational self-interest to impersonate public policy, it becomes a social degenerate. They become social degenerates because in those moments, they lessen a collective's ability to become more. When the legitimacy of organizations and institutions are called into question, organizational pride has a tendency to not identify organizational responsibility as much as it seeks to justify its existence. In this way, prideful institutions and individuals share a similar culpability; they both prioritize approaches and behaviors that work to promote self-interest at the expense of the public. In the case of individuals, there are a series of options that collectives can employ that can compel the compliance of the individual. However, the options for the individual to grieve the institution are less frequent and those that exist tend to be complex and cumbersome.

The dangers of pride as a social degenerate are many and vary in impact. However, few individual prideful acts and occurrences have the potential to suborn the salacious and duplicitous corrosive impact on society as prideful institutions that operate against the interest of public good. Prideful individuals, institutions and organization are degenerates because they erode the collective confidence necessary for trust and toleration of individual and organizational flaws and mistakes. Moreover, collective aspiration provides the framework and prism to accept individual acquiescence in the face of self-interest. In the end, it matters not if the subject of analysis is the individual or an institution, when pride works as a subjugator of social aspiration, it not only makes the collective less, it more solemnly can call into question the legitimate existence of the collective altogether.

What are some Appropriate Responses?

Pride is a complicated phenomenon to respond to because of its ubiquitous presence in both our society and our hearts. It is almost a natural tendency for either an individual or an institution to seek its worth as a side effect of trying to understand and realize its function and purpose. Pride is in part a mechanism to flesh out one's worth and pride is in part an overestimation of that worth. Individuals and institutions have to remain diligent to revisiting their sense of value in the context of the purposeful action and collective aspiration. There is almost no way to avoid the consequences that often accompany mistakes, imperfections, expectations and disappointments.

The natural outcomes are struggles with inadequacy, wayward purpose development and overcompensation. Each of these outcomes has its own dangers; inadequacy, the feeling of never being able to do enough and the response tends to be to do far more than is necessary and in essence, doing too much. Pride suggests under these circumstances, individual action alone has power to make the necessary improvements for the collective, and rarely is that the case. As a result, the unnecessary action ultimately serves the interest of the actor's insecurities rather than as a function to promote and develop collective aspiration. The development of a wayward purpose has its central danger in constructing a sense of meaning through one's imperfections and inadequacies.

Pride under these circumstances, has the power to influence the manner in which one sees the self. Often times, this vision has little or nothing to do with the aspirations of the collective but more about how the actor (individuals or institutions) seeks acknowledgment of contribution, purpose and intention with relatively little or no concern for the collective impact. In fact, pride often reinforces this wayward purpose in the face of grievance from the affected parties. In this case, pride feeds the intention of the actor despite the consequences that have been availed by the affected parties. In this process, the collective is in danger in part because the perceived action to protect the collective is on the contrary, threatening it.

Overcompensation remains a constant danger in this scenario because pride distorts both what is perceived as the function of the actor and what lengths to which the actor is willing to go

DR. ERIC L. JOHNSON

to bring into existence what is believed to be in the interest of public good. In this case, pride gives permission for an individual actor to implicitly lose faith in the collective's ability to survive and thrive under perceived potential dangers and simultaneously gives permission to the actor to do what is believed to be necessary to bring out the desired outcome. In this case, pride invites one to assume responsibilities that extend beyond one's capacity but more importantly, it compromises the balance of shared responsibility that ultimately serves as the foundation for the collective's existence. The responses of the collective to these subtle but critical challenges to the collective aspiration are few and complicated at best. Any tactical response has to meet the strategic goal of a deep commitment to extending individual capacity by utilization of collective aspiration.

Many institutions undergo periodic institutional reviews for this stated purpose. However, most individuals are absent of a similar process and it may be helpful to incorporate such mechanisms in one's lived experience. However, periodic reviews are not particularly useful if they are not understood in the context of the central contract that every collective operates within. The idea that each individual is better because the collective exists. Any appropriate response by an institution or individual has to have that as the guiding principle to re-establish or maintain any order perceived to be legitimate.

Chapter V

PRIDE WORKS AGAINST THE SELF

*"Notions of self, pride, and spirit
are deeply complicated, contested
and subjective ideas."*

DR. ERIC L. JOHNSON

How does Pride impact the Self Spiritually?

Notions of self, pride and spirit are deeply complicated, contested and subjective ideas. Any one of them has the potential to invite dissent, disagreement and intense passion, physical and otherwise. How do we understand the self when so much of it remains unrevealed, unconscious and misunderstood? Most of the journey we call life is in part a revelation of different aspects of the self through experience, learning, prayer, meditation, time and a host of other factors not mentioned. Who or what the self is remains in many ways a mystery. This is particularly true given that the meaning of self is constantly under investigation and evolution. Here, the spiritual self is not so much a reference to a Supreme Being/Life Force or God as many would prefer, although that is certainly not irrelevant and for some, it is critically essential. Rather, the spiritual self here refers to those aspects of the human identity that cannot be captured by observations in the mirror.

It is analogous to the difference between the brain and the mind. Both refer to the organ housed in the human skull but they do not mean the same thing. Brain refers to the mechanics and components of the organ, identifying functions of different sectors of the brain as such. In essence, brain refers to the scientific understandings of what is now understood about the role of the organ. However, mind tends to refer to the mysterious and amazing operation of the organ that includes the "awe and wonder" of its abilities. The mind is not simply about the functions of the organ but it also includes the relationship between the organ and the rest of the body and spirit. Mind also refers to the capacity of the organ and its almost limitless potential. It includes the amazing adaptations and skills that only appear when they are necessary. Investigation of the mind involves an ever present humility in that, what we think we understand about it is continuingly expanding.

Pride works against the spiritual self because it limits both the access and capacity of the spiritual self because much of the spiritual self is revealed only when necessary, often during times of doubt, crisis, and/or sober reflection. Pride presents a danger to limit the frequency of those occurrences. Pride not only has the potential to limit the frequency of the occurrences, it also taints the quality of each event because it comprises one's ability to submit to the process. Pride tends to find its relevancy and strength in the so called rational and conscious self. As such, pride has a tendency to see the unconscious and unrevealed spiritual self as a potential threat. Pride works to limit both its access and influence on one's development. As the spiritual self seeks to find and open doors for revelation, pride seeks to limit the opening of those same doors and when possible, it seeks to close, lock and conveniently misplace the key. Pride's impact on the spiritual self is significant in that its goal is containment at all cost and when possible, destroys it.

How does Pride Impact the Self Mentally?

The mind remains an important and convoluted aspect of what is often identified as the human self. The mental construction of one's reality cannot be overstated. Biologically, humans, for survival, have attempted to mentally survey their environment, to predict potential dangers, identify critical necessities and plan the pursuit of coveted desires. Despite the historical evolution of both humans and their environment, the need for the mental self to achieve those goals has changed very little. Successfully predicting potential dangers requires an awareness and acknowledgement of vulnerabilities and inadequacies that are often hidden by pride. Pride has a tendency to provide assurances when caution is probably more prudent. Successfully accepting the dangers in an environment is a challenge for pride because it requires one to expend mental energy in exploring unanticipated occurrences and preparation for action to circumstances previously not seen or understood. Mental growth is largely an outcome of learning from mistakes and pride is sometimes reticent to acknowledge them.

When humans are seeking to identify critical needs, pride has both the power and influence to distort the distinction between wants and needs. How one distinguishes between wants and needs serves as an instrument of evaluation on almost every aspect of one's life. The extent to which one is willing to go for a want distorted as a need or vice versa, gives some insight into the mental perception of one's self. Even the questions we ask about perceived critical needs give some information about the mental self. Relevant questions are: What do we understand to be a critical necessity? How do we prioritize competing critical necessities? How do fulfilling critical necessities impact the perception of the self?

The mental development of one's perceived self is often predicated on the processing of previous experiences, mistakes and understandings. Mental development is complicated by pride because it has a tendency to misrepresent mistakes as successes and mislead one to understand psychological and physical pleasures and comforts as critical necessities. Moreover, pride has the ability to compel one to spend disproportionate amounts of time planning the pursuit of coveted desires. Indeed, pride in fact has the power to construct a lens of reality where the planning for coveted desires is often falsely understood as exploring one's higher self. A clear distinction between the two can be determined by the motivating energy. Does one seek a peace paid for by doing the work to make one's self better or does one seek a pleasure to alleviate an anxiety one has about her or his-self or about the world they perceive? This is a question that each of us has to address if we aspire to examine the role of pride in our pursuit of a better self.

The mental development of the self is a highly subjective enterprise that requires humility to be aware of not just what we think we know but more importantly, it also entails an awareness of what we don't know. A quintessential question to address is: How to account for not knowing what we don't know? Pride has a way of compelling the self to hallucinate a world where that question has no place. As such, the impact of pride on the self mentally is largely contingent on each of our insecurities, inadequacies, perceived critical needs and coveted desires.

How does Pride Impact the Imagination?

The impact of pride on the imagination is profoundly relevant. How do we identify the capacity of human potential? Almost every time the capacity of the human potential has been identified, it has been exceeded. Pride has the propensity to place limits when in all actuality, there are none? The ability of the human imagination has proven to be the greatest weapon ever designed to combat danger and concurrently, the single biggest destructive force ever seen. It is the human imagination that envisioned the possibility to chart the stars and to explore other galaxies. It is the human imagination that seeks to explore the deep and often times, dark psychological recesses of the human mind. For scientists, the imagination is the place where the cure for cancer is currently housed.

For Theologians, Priests, Pastors, Rabbis and other spiritual trekkers, the imagination represents a gateway to perceive that part of the universe not bound by human understanding. For children, imagination is a preliminary place to travel, where they can discover purpose and meaning. For every human being, imagination represents everything we could be but are not. It is not entirely inconceivable that the imagination is where the Divine stores the purpose of each soul. Pride often requests that the imagination be less active so that there can be more answers present and ensure that it remains as relevant as possible. As we imagine our capacity to learn, pride compels us to determine what we know. As the imagination encourages us to conceive of what could happen, pride constrains the self to examine what has happened. Where imagination offers the self-excitement, jubilation and exploration, pride offers pessimism, anxiety and fear of the unknown.

What imagination offers the self can in no way be substituted by pride because where imagination offers progress, pride offers stagnation and status quo. How does the self-utilize the imagination more and rely on pride less? In that question is the difference between living in our potential and dwelling on our failures. In that question is the power to forgive or the permission to not. Imagination is in part a mechanism to move us from where we are to where we want to be. It has the energy to reveal that aspect of our identity most necessary when we are supremely challenged.

What should we do about it?

The idea that pride works against the self is a complicated notion in that it is the self that constructs, nurtures and sustains it. How is it possible that the self produces something that has the wherewithal to destroy it? Is that counter intuitive? Indeed it is but it is no less true. In the same way that cancer cells are typically the result of the body's natural production process, pride is a natural result of the self's process to determine worth. When cancerous cells continue to grow and violate the natural life cycle of the cell, they leave less space for the new cells and maybe more importantly, they mercenarily consume the nutrients for all cells disproportionately for themselves.

Prideful ideas and notions venally occupy the heart and mind of the human identity at the expense of other inklings and appreciations to the extent that the self is severely compromised.

We are as far from solving or preventing the growth of prideful ideas as we are from relieving the body from the result of cancerous tumors. Like cancer, under certain circumstances, we can work to put our prideful approaches in remission but we when do, we have to be ever wary of the cancer's potential return and be primed to begin a response with urgent dynamism. Pride's cancerous effect on the development of the self mentally, spiritually and emotionally is a call to bring into our life's activities that requires us to explore areas of self-development. Ideas that invite an awareness to account for not knowing what we don't know. Activities that give other non-prideful ideas the nutrients they need to survive while simultaneously providing a natural life cycle for prideful ideas to live and die. Each human has to do that for him or herself, there is no prescribed protocol and a prognosis cannot be given. The best defense offered to date is an observant and cautious approach to self-development and an awareness of prideful growths in human understanding. No one can be offered guarantees and upon further reflection, maybe no one should be.

Chapter VI

PRIDE, AN ACQUAINTANCE TO MALEVOLENCE

*"As acquaintances pride and malevolence
on occasion share the same space and when they
do they feed one another's worst attributes,
which is a scenario welcomed by both."*

How does Pride Differ from Malevolence?

Prideful enterprises often have a latent and an implicitly aggressive nature toward others. Pride more often than not gives permission to be primarily concerned with the identified interests of the actor. While pride at best has a subtle hostility for any act or event outside the perceived interest of the actor and at worst, pride gives permission for unveiled open assaults and attacks. However, pride alone rarely has as the end goal the intent of inflicting harm. Pride wishes only to have its way and most often it will employ the path of least resistance. Certainly, that does not mean pride has any necessary aversion to inflicting harm because often times, injury is an outcome of prideful industry. However, it is possible to execute the interests and will of prideful agents while minimizing the damage done to others in the process.

Malevolence on the other hand is often related to the willful intent to inflict harm. In fact, malevolence refers to not only any resulting wounds but it also includes any spite that served as a motivating force. There are those who understand malevolence to operate with such ill will that it is synonymous with unadulterated evil. Pride differs from malevolence in some fairly important areas. While pride tends to give much attention to the self and its interest, malevolent actions tend to center around people and things outside the self. More importantly, malevolence is often absent of a specific and defined outcome. Where pride often works to express a desire and realize a certain result, malevolence can operate in many forms, inflicting chaos and pain at a target because the injury is the purpose. While it is possible for a malevolent intent to concentrate around a specific target, it acts with much less precision and easily redirects its ill will with a frequency that makes it unpredictable at best and at worst, it appears to be completely random.

To the extent that on occasion, pride's appetite can be temporarily sated, malevolence has no such reality. Each malicious act creates the craving for the next. The more harmful and injurious the result, the more malice seeks to increase its scope. While both pride and malevolence can be ruinous, they differ in their desired capacity; where malice feeds off the resulting destruction, pride on the contrary needs an audience to admire its work. The connection between pride and malevolence has no redeeming qualities and where they acquaint is a place that most should avoid as either a spectator or a participant.

Why are Pride and Malevolence Acquainted?

Every relationship at its essence requires clarity of its function. The more clear the function, the stronger the relationship. In close relationships, the clarity of function is fixed, valued and understood by all parties. In less close relationships, clarity is compromised for a variety of reasons. When the function of the relationship is complex or portable, then it only comes into relevancy when it is called upon. Friends and some family members often represent close relationships that have functions that are fixed, valued and understood. Conversely, acquaintances are less close because the function of the relationship is less understood, valued and fixed. The function of an acquaintance is both temporal and contextual in nature, making clarity difficult. Moreover, if time and setting are important elements to the function of an acquaintance, its value can never be fixed. Friends are valued all the time and acquaintances are valued only when they are.

Pride and malevolence are acquainted because of their connection to the propensity to inflict harm. The value each has for the other is temporal and contextual at best. There are times when pride wants to provide malevolence with a needed target and a sense of direction while malevolence wants to provide pride with a welcomed method to achieve its determined goals. In which case, the temporal and contextual requirements are met. Temporally, the timing of these occasions represents an unholy opportunity to wreak mischief and harm. The context is often a barrier because malevolence often does not welcome the direction offered by pride, because it often seeks to institute destruction at every opportunity. Pride resists this notion not for any other purpose other than its own vanity.

As with all acquaintances, pride and malevolence do have much in common. Their acquaintance can be detrimental for anyone who happens to be in their company. The familiarity of these two principles can be deceptively subtle. The presence of one often represents an opportunity for the other to find a purpose. While certainly malevolence has its own unique space, concerns and presence, pride often times provides a connection to malevolence that is often nuanced but nonetheless direct. As acquaintances, pride and malevolence on occasion share the same space and when they do, they feed one another's worst attributes, which is a scenario welcomed by both. Indeed, these two are acquainted because when they are together, they are more powerful than when they are alone. The primary purpose for each is the justification for their own existence; something each has for the other in a way that few other factors do.

Important Things to Consider

Malevolence is something that many adamantly deny having in their hearts. Indeed, most would be correct when referring to the most extreme expressions of it. While malevolence is something that has intent to inflict harm, it is not simply about the resulting injury. It is as much about the intent as it is about the result. When one intends to bring harm to another and they are not successful in the outcome, they are no less malicious for the intent. Too often, malevolence is conveniently understood in the context of the outcome not for the spiteful energy that served as its motivator. It is important to note that the outcome has little to do with the presence of malice or not. If one were to inflict terrible harm without intent, is that malice? The answer is probably not. But if one were to wish grave injury to another without a resulting outcome, is that less malicious? Unfortunately, the answer is still probably not as well. The complicated thing about true malice is that it most often requires the presence of an honor system where one has to self-report for a true and accurate measurement. Malevolence is not in the act as many of us would conveniently like it to be, it is in the heart. It is difficult to discern the intent of the actor from the result, however, it is not completely impossible either.

Only the actor can truly disclose the presence of malicious intent or malevolence in one's heart. Because of that, many of us are shielded from being forced to unveil any malice we may be concealing in our hearts. This concealment would not be without a price because all the space dedicated to storing malice could be used to house all the goodness that often gets left unnoticed. Is it malevolent only when one operates with spite or hatred? What is it when one simply does not care what happens? What is it when one had no intent and no direct relationship with a detrimental outcome but is nonetheless contented? Whatever the answers are to those questions, they are not benevolent in any way, shape or fashion. Dr. Martin Luther King Jr. has been quoted as saying "all that is necessary for evil to rein is for good people to do nothing." Leaving the question: Is being contented with detrimental outcomes absent of malice when you are not an actor or when they don't affect you? The question of malevolence in the human experience and heart is one not as easily answered as it may appear.

Chapter VII

PRIDE, A SUBJUGATOR OF JOY

*"Moreover, pride is perfectly suited
to be a subjugator of joy because it proposes
to answer all the questions that joy cannot."*

Subjugation as a Social Concept

The human spirit naturally seeks a path of freedom and growth and it does so until it is subjugated by the coercive propensity of conformity. While conformity has its merits, it is often in opposition to individual self-expression. Because the human spirit naturally seeks to be free and to grow, the conformity frequently required by society is realized at a significant cost. This would be an unfortunate and sad occurrence if the subject was one spirit but indeed, the subject of analysis here is most. Every society that has ever existed has necessitated some amount of conformity to sustain its existence. Without question, conformity more often than not, is in the interest of the individual as well. So how does the, albeit, unnatural act of conformity take on the detrimental attributes of subjugation? When do group expectations act as strong-arm tactics to drive and compel individual acquiescence? How is it possible to have so many spirits imprison themselves when they have access to the key? These are important questions to be considered on the topic of subjugation.

At its essence, subjugation refers to control and governance. How does one distinguish the required act of group governance from coercive subjugation? When do any group's expectations serve to subjugate its members and others' potentials? The navigation of these two areas may be more complicated than many would like to admit. An important concept to this equation is the notion of agency. To what extent does the group governance incorporate the agency of the affected individuals? Agency here refers to the active and ongoing negotiation between the individual and the group about both the method of governance and the overall understanding of the intentions of the governing body. When there is a breakdown in either the understanding of intentions or the method, then there is more subjugation than governance. The extent of the subjugation is in direct proportion to the extent of the breakdown.

In the mix of a perceived subjugation, the restraint of human expression becomes pressurized. The pressure accumulating scientifically seeks release and often times it erupts, not unlike what happens when you remove the cap from a shaken carbonated beverage. The eruption often lacks direction or reason. Whatever is in the path of the eruption is affected and most certainly, when the cap is removed from the shaken carbonated beverage, a clean-up is almost always required. Subjugation is a pressurizing element to one person or to any number of them; if there is subjugation, there is need for a release of the pressure. In the case of subjugation, there are two plausible responses. Ensure that the negotiation of the governed is as active as possible and ensure that the necessary pressure releases are present and considerately managed. However, subjugation and pressurization is far more likely in the absence of joy. Joy has inherently all the tools necessary to address subjugation.

The Nature of Joy

If the nature of joy could be summed up in a single word, it would be to appreciate. While joy is often understood in the context of happiness, joy is not happy. While happy is an antonym for sad, joy is an appreciation of the worthiness that both concepts have in a lived experience. Joy is not pleasure or absent pain as happy is often described. Joy is an appreciation for the meaningful struggles that are often encountered that makes one better than they would have been. Joy is an appreciation for the meaning that pain provides in our moments of pleasure. In addition, Joy is awareness that when events unfold in way that was neither predicted nor welcomed, it is so for our greater good even when understanding is absent.

The nature of joy is to appreciate the gift of life when circumstances are such that one can be inclined to not do so. Joy represents the ability to love and like one self during sober moments of reflection and evaluation of one's flaws and inadequacies. Joy uniquely provides the possibility to be acutely aware of life's many drudgeries and instantaneously foresee Divine opportunity. Dictionary explanations of joy are often incomplete. Most refer to a sense of well-being or good fortune and problematically, many include happy as part of the explanation for joy. Certainly, there is a pleasure source included in joy but it also includes peace and serenity that in all things, there is reason to be hopeful. Joy is in part a spiritual decision to see beyond temporary circumstances and setbacks, to understand that dawn appears only after the darkest part of the day. Joy includes happy but it is more than happy in the same way that despair includes sadness but certainly, despair is more than just sadness. Despair includes a sense of hopelessness for which sadness simply does not account.

In that way, Joy includes a sense of perseverance, recognition and awareness of one's reality for which happy simply does not account. Joy includes the ability to be appreciative in moments of profound pain, hurt and sadness. A comprehensive clarification that distinguishes Joy from happy is not entirely rational but indeed, it is the irrational belief that in the darkest moments of one's life, there is reason to be appreciative and that is one element that makes joy a unique occurrence in the human experience. Joy includes the possibility to be at our worst or at least, in very dire circumstances and perceive how as a result of persevering, one will be better because all things work out for the good even when the rational explanation is beyond our comprehension. Joy is the reason that one can find to cry from sadness and laugh in appreciation at the same time. An appreciation of true joy requires a submission to the inadequacy of one's own individual understanding and it requires a humility that most simply refuses to operate within.

Joy is in conflict with the human tendency to want to know or explain. The more joy is present in one's life, the more one has to trust in things that are not rational and yet unseen. There are those who call that trust faith but in any event, joy is in part a subtle perception that the vast majority of the things happening in one's life are not under any rational control that any of us have. While the notion of faith is a concept that many resist for a host of reasons, hope is a concept to which many can subscribe. However, there are those who believe that control is something they can have and they seek to have it. For them, anxiety is an accepted companion and pride is a potential confidant.

Pride, a Subjugator of Joy

Containment and control are the goals of any good subjugator. Pride is exceedingly good at containment because it learns to anticipate the moves of its prey. Moreover, pride is perfectly suited to be a subjugator of joy because it proposes to answer all the questions that joy cannot. How can one be assured that when it appears that all is lost, that everything will be ok? Why should one be appreciative in the face of profound pain and hurt? How can one are assured that giving of oneself results in a desired outcome? When a result is not desired or welcomed and struggle is a foreseeable reality, what reason does one have to be grateful? Can anyone be guaranteed a specific outcome when a particular input has been invested?

Joy is at a complete disadvantage when faced with such critically important questions to which the spirit often demands answers. The humility necessary to appreciate joy is uncommon because of what it costs to possess it. The cost to possess true joy is the end to the perceived and subtle attitude that explanations are owed and can be developed and determined. The cost includes doing your best in the darkness and operating in the trust that whatever happens does so for a reason and the explanation may never be revealed. In the face of that almost overpowering and overwhelming reality, pride steps in to provide answers. In the midst of the darkness, pride seeks to provide some light. It matters not to most that the light offered is not sunlight, instead, it is a bright reflection on the tonsil of a throat that seeks to swallow us whole.

Pride offers assurances that joy frankly cannot. As such, it is not at all a mystery why many would willingly follow the false light rather than accept the ambiguity necessitated by joy. Joy cannot offer an outcome. It can only appreciate a process. Maybe that is as it should be; maybe true joy should have a remarkable cost so that its presence is a tremendous message to those who have it and those who don't. Every time we seek to answer questions that deep in our heart we know are unanswerable, we give joy less room to work and expand pride's workshop. When we do so, we give pride all the tools necessary to subjugate joy but know every time we do it, it costs our spirit the room to be free and grow. Pride is perfectly suited to subjugate joy because it masquerades as a helpful element, providing clues to solve a riveting mystery when in all actuality, it is a jailer dropping bread crumbs that will lead us to our would be cage.

Pride subjugates joy in the worst way in that it robs one of the ability to appreciate the precious gift that is life. The ups, downs, pleasure, pains, disappointments and excitements all represent the full capacity of the human experience and all of which serve to provide meaning that would be absent if any one of them were missing. When pride is successful in subjugating joy, and that is often by the way, it serves to undercut the very essence of what it means to be here. Joy in part is the appreciation for having life and experiencing it in all its wondrous dimensions. However, joy is not an accident. It is the deliberate decision to be fully present in every moment that one has the opportunity to experience.

When pride subjugates one's joy, it is because one chose the false light, not because something bad happened.

Pride, you can't have my Joy

The most interesting phenomenon about pride's subjugation of joy is that it requires both complicity and surrender. Pride presents itself as strength when in all actuality, it is weakness. To be relevant, pride relies on a tacit acquiescence to withdraw from the battle. Joy is the strength and resolves to march on no matter the circumstance. Joy recognizes struggle as nourishment that feeds the spirit. In the unending battle with pride, there will be moments of defeat and surrender. Pride's insurgence on the human spirit is ruthlessly tenacious and as a result, one is always at risk of becoming battle weary. A soldier is brave not because they win the battle but because they fight the battle regardless of the odds. In fact, the more lopsided the battle, the more bravery that is required. Joy is the bravery required to fully claim the prize of a well lived life. Humanity's battle with pride is epic and each of us is participants whether we want to be or not. Joy stands tall in the presence of pride and is amused with pride's constant attempts at suppression.

When one is fully present and appreciative of the presence of grace and mercy, pride is reduced to little more than the irritation of a gnat. Prides gains strength in the absence of joy and as a result, its preoccupation with suppression is for its own survival. When pride seeks to subjugate joy, it does so for its own existence. When joy reminds us what is present, it is pride that points out what is absent. When joy reminds what we have, pride highlights what we want. When joy accepts what is, pride whispers what it should be. When joy wants to appreciate the light, pride accentuates the impact of the brightness. Joy is both the willingness and perseverance to carry on, while pride is permission to surrender? The battle with pride should not be underestimated, however, in no uncertain terms, it should be understood that triumph is always possible. All that is necessary to claim victory is the attitude, words and approach that boldly roars "pride, you can't have my joy".

Chapter VIII

PRIDE, A CONTRIVANCE OF INEFFECTIVE PARENTS

*"An interesting question is:
Are there common elements of
parenting that exist across culture,
religion, and even species?"*

The Role of Parents Visited

What is the function of a parent? How should parental duties be understood and performed? These are questions that are not easily answered. There are a plethora of sources that inform questions like these for every family. The religious and cultural context of a family plays a significant role in the effort to answer such questions. However, these questions are not confined to the human experience, every organism that produces offspring in some way, shape, or fashion responds to the same issues. An interesting question is: Are there common elements of parenting that exist across the culture, religion and even species? It would seem that the one factor across all parenting context is the seemingly instinctive obligation to provide offspring with the necessary tools to promote their survival.

In this effort, some animals move in herds while others hide their offspring in inconspicuous places. Some even have their offspring in gaudy numbers so as to increase the likelihood of survival for some. It would seem that humans use some form of all of these methods. From predator to prey, parents attempt to protect offspring from as many dangers as possible. There are no contexts where parents are 100% successful at protecting the young from harm. As a result, in every context, parents attempt to construct a setting that gives their offspring the best chance for survival. Because the dangers are real and the stakes are oftentimes life and death, parents attempt to anticipate dangers both known and unknown. In the human context of parenting, physical survival is not the only aspect of protection that presents concern. Human offspring require emotional, psychological and for many, spiritual protection.

While these elements can be as important as physical protection, they are far more complicated to achieve. How do human parents ensure that the emotional, psychological and spiritual protection they provide meets the needs of their offspring? What are the sources that should be referenced to bring about the desired outcome? How do parents account for their own shortcomings in all the areas mentioned to ensure that the protection provided is as healthy as possible? It is not clear that other species have a sense of spiritual self that has to be both nurtured and developed. It would also seem that individual emotional development and psychological identity development are more complex in human communities that in others but that may not be entirely accurate. Primates, elephants and even lions are among some species that appear to have both emotional and psychological dispositions that in many ways, mirror human circumstances.

Certainly, every species seems to have some unique elements about parenting that are unique to the species but certainly, there also appears to be some aspects that are consistent. One of which is the almost innate desire to pass on to offspring the necessary tools for survival. The question becomes, how much can any parent know about the totality of the offspring's existence and thereby leaving a significant margin of error. It would seem the more variables added to the child rearing process, the more opportunities there are to get it wrong.

Pride and Child Rearing

While parenting seems to be implicitly focused on the actions of the parents, child rearing intuitively has its relevancy on child development. How does a parent provide the best environment possible to nurture the growth of children? How does one explain when children have the observable best of everything and make surprising little of it? In comparison, how is it possible for some children to experience challenges that would compromise most adults and do well in life anyway? If any one of us could answer those questions, how different would life be? While certainly there are factors that most would agree should and should not be present in a child's life, however, that alone does not explain any particular outcome. If child rearing is the training and nurturing of children, then how do parents both account and overcome the shortcomings from their own childhood?

If parents like any other humans are affected and shaped by both the good and bad experiences of their own childhood, how do parents operate beyond their own inadequacies? How does child rearing account for all the things we think are good for children but prove to have a different effect? Too often, parents substitute control for learning opportunities and forsake learning opportunities for control, motivated by the desire to implement safety protocols. It is not even conceivably possible to ever get it right all the time and getting it right most of the time is a tall order that many strive for but few achieve. Child rearing is a critically important event in the life of all humans who embark on the journey, however, almost no one is prepared to encounter the twist and turns that are often presented. The complexity of emotional development is an anxiety producing aspect of the process all by itself.

When one inserts identity development, spiritual health and the general cruelties of the world, child rearing in thought becomes something unthinkably complex. The least prepared is the parent who believes they have all these aspects under control. Pride can invite one to think that they have answers about child rearing to questions that have not been asked yet. While child rearing presents a plethora of unknowns and answerable questions, pride invites one to believe that what they don't know, they can know. An idea that is not entirely irrational, that notion often provides support in situations that present significant challenges. However, in the case of child rearing, that approach lacks the humility necessary to survive what can seem to be an onslaught of unforeseen and unwelcomed occurrences that can sometimes require a re-evaluation of reality. Child rearing has no shortage of experts that spend their lives attempting to understand what circumstances are necessary to produce the best possible outcome.

Certainly, parents should consult the best information available on the journey but no expert can know your specific circumstances, understand your experiences or reconcile your shortcomings. In the end, that is a matter left to each parent. However complex child rearing happens to be, most parents and children survive it but rarely without the scars and wounds that mark important opportunities to grow. When pride is given less opportunity to operate, we can summon the humility to grow in real time. Facilitating the possibility to replace wounds and scars with the wisdom gained from growth opportunities. It is not possible to develop preconceived answers to unpredictable questions, as such; child rearing requires the discipline to commit to a learning process that involves both parents and children.

Pride and Discipline

Discipline is an interesting concept when connected to child rearing and parenting. For some parents, the subject mostly has to do with consequences and punishment. For other parents, discipline has to do with a commitment to follow a particular order or a set of rules. Still some parents see discipline as a mechanism to establish parental control in the child rearing process. Intriguingly, most of those references to discipline are simply a means to a particular end but the question is, to what end? The presence of consequences and punishment are in part a signal to understand some broader lesson. Furthermore, following the rules is supposed to present the possibility and opportunity of achieving one's goals and dreams. However, any semblance of parental control that can be exhibited in the child rearing process is quickly challenged by the broader society. While the notion of discipline is ubiquitous in most approaches to child rearing, there are still questions as to the function it should have in the process.

Certainly, each parent will explore this challenge in a way that best suits the context of their parenting approach. Parents who understand discipline as a process to train and mold the development of their children probably see discipline as something that probably includes all the identified elements and probably more not mentioned. However, few parents understand discipline should probably involve a parental commitment to growth in unpredictable and dynamic situations. In theory, discipline is a mechanism that allows for the optimum circumstances necessary to promote growth and development. Discipline is not a means unto itself. However, the aspect of discipline that is emphasized in a particular context is one of a parent's choosing. Parents are left to decide on one approach best for all situations or should discipline approaches be fluid to respond to unpredictable and dynamic circumstances. There are no clear answers and right and wrong are subject to the result. If parents are getting the results they want, then maybe it's right and if parents are not getting the results they wanted, then maybe a different approach or emphasis is warranted.

However, anyone who purports to have the answers is claiming to have access to the future. Who among us can truly claim that with any legitimate authority? Pride is perilous in this context because it can invite parents to play Russian roulette with their children's development. Pride can suggest answers when questions are probably more prudent. The risk and reward are so critical that as parents, pride is an ever present risk. Mistakes parents make can have lasting effects on the development of the children and not recognizing that potential can be a grave mistake. Pride operates in such a way that it can suggest that the limitations of a parent's understanding is enough for their children's development and rarely is that the case. Discipline does not allow parents to predict an environment's risk factors but pride can sometimes coerce a parent into operating with that assumption.

Discipline can be most effective when parents approach it as a method of operation in unknown and unknowable circumstances. Pride can make it less likely that parents recognize what they don't know and thereby losing an opportunity for growth for both the parent and the child. To the extent that parents approach child rearing in a way that growth opportunities are lessened, they increase the probability of teaching their children to do the same. Pride is a luxury that most parents can't afford. It can leave children in situations that appear to satisfy our desire for safety, while potentially being perilous beyond a parent's worst nightmare.

Pride and Ineffective Parenting

What is effective parenting? A question that troubles a great deal of parents. How can a parent determine the future consequences of actions done in the present? Parenting is an arena that brings into relevancy every major belief one has about the world and life. Without exception, parenting includes all of one's vulnerabilities, insecurities and fears. As humans attempt to answer and address profound questions about life, we add to it the cadre of unanswerable questions, what it means to be an effective parent. Pride is a challenge because deep down in the conscious of many parents, they want to believe they are doing the right thing for their children. What parent wouldn't reasonably want to believe that they were doing the right thing by their children?

Pride has the power to provide such assurances even when it is not warranted. For sure, one of the most difficult things for parents of any species is to accept that they do not have total control of the environment in which their offspring operates.

On occasion, ineffective human parents attempt to insert routine and discipline as a mechanism of control to provide the facsimile of safety but yet it is not. Pride not only can have an impact on the way parents love their children, it can also frame the entire circumstance which parents construct to relate to them. How does one arrive at the understanding of what is an effective parent? If children reach adulthood in relative good health, does that meet the benchmark of effective parenting? Each parent that exists or has ever existed has a unique combination of experiences, values, beliefs, goals and concerns that makes effective parenting at the very least a fluid and relative concept.

Many parents use as a benchmark, the life choices of their adult children. However, that is at the very least complex because many of the choices that children make during late adolescence and early adulthood are in part a result of their own experiences with the world but certainly, the contributions of a parent are never irrelevant. If effective parenting is the result of producing an intended outcome, then how does one evaluate outcomes that were not directly intended? Is it possible to be an ineffective parent even when your children's life choices are well adaptive and productive if a parent's contributions to those choices are minimal? If a parent gives all the best things to children and the children make counterproductive choices in adolescence and early adulthood, is that an ineffective parent? In either case, one complexity is that the assessment is removed from the action. If the result is the marker, then the question is not effective parenting. It is how were children parented? If effective parenting is the goal, then parents have to consistently assess both their performance and the development of their children.

Effective parenting requires every parent to constantly ask the question, are they producing the result they intended? This question is relevant every day of the parenting experience; in every stage of development of a child's life. Effective parenting requires parents to explicitly determine their desired outcome and determine if that is what is happening. Ineffective parenting is probably relevant to any set of circumstances that was not directly intended by the caretaker or parent. It is difficult to be effective when parents have not determined the objective. Pride is a danger because it gives permission to ask the question less than a parent should. Sometimes, parents are not prepared for the work it takes to be effective and as a result, pride fills the gap. When effective parents encounter a challenge, they have to determine the goal or re-assess the current one. Ineffective parents get permission from pride to determine what they have done is all they can do.

Pride pretends to be the first aid to heal wounds when it is actually a bacterium that allows wounds to get infected and does more damage than if the right questions had been asked and the proper treatment administered. Ineffective parenting has a limitless number of presentations because every parent has a different story and effective parenting is not a recipe. It is an approach and a commitment to growth. Effective parenting can be produced out of a great deal of hardship and pain while ineffective parenting can be the result of material contentment and worldly satisfaction. Every parent is obliged to determine what each looks like in their parenting context. The important point here is that pride provides permission to shortcut the work of effective parenting to the detriment of children, parents and society.

Chapter IX

PRIDE, THE INVERSE OF INTELLECT

"Pride is a masterful illusionist and the smarter one is the more illusions pride has at its disposal."

The Nature of Intellect

Most often, intellect refers to the capacity of the mind to understand, learn or know. Intellect at its essence invites cerebral exploration. Intellect is less about what one knows and more about how one is driven to expand one's capacity to think. The production of knowledge has no limitation and one's intellect has to ever expand to incorporate an almost infinite number of possibilities that continue to find ways to populate. Intellect not only refers to what one knows or understands, but it also accounts for one's pursuit of intellectual growth. Often times, when intellect is the topic of discussion, words and concepts like reason, knowledge and rational are used in the explanation. However, it is just as appropriate to use terms like awe, wonder, curiosity or humility.

True intellect is in part the understanding that what is thought to be known represents only a small fraction of what is possible to be understood. The pursuit of intellectual growth is in part a desire and commitment to expand and enhance the intellectual capabilities of one's mind. However, this quest is not an academic endeavor that serves only the purpose of the pursuit itself. The pursuit of intellectual engagement exist in part as an avenue for humanity to fulfill its obligation to be better and grow to our individual and collective best self. Moreover, all understanding represents a temporal existence that is completely contingent on fragile assumptions often made with extremely limited information. While temporary and faulty assumptions will forever be a part of any intellectual enterprise that includes humans, it is not the outcome that provides the meaning for such ventures. It is the process to grow that serves as the most important component of such exercises.

Intellectual pursuit also serves as a reminder of both the insignificant and indispensable role humanity plays in universal possibilities. Smart as a notion is sometimes seen as a synonym to intellect but there *are* differences that make these two ideas discernibly different. As a comparison, quick and fast are related but they are not the same thing. Quick refers to sudden moves that happen over shorter periods of time. Fast refers to a sustained set of advancements over much longer periods of time. As a result, it is possible to be quick and not very fast. However, it is also possible to be quick and fast. Intellect and Smart have a similar relationship. Smart is most relevant in particular situations. Intellect refers to a way of being in the world that uses one's mind as a method to process everything perceived. Smart refers to knowledge one demonstrates in one or more areas. Often, smart is something that can be developed with time and experience. Intellect is less about the demonstration and more about a method of processing. Similar to quick and fast, it is possible to have intellect and not be what is often referred to as smart because there is an absence of applying ideas to real world practicality. Intellect is not simply what one does or says, intellect is more about how one approaches their world. Intellect is a means by which the mind's capacity is expanded; smart is the mechanism by which one applies ideas in a specific context.

The distinction is relevant because intellect is a source of growth internally, smart is a more about quick witted ideas that may have substance or not. Smart does not require one to pursue anything. In fact, smart can operate as a barrier because it often serves the purpose one has for it. Smart and intellect can be at odds because one requires us to commit to it and the other allows us to commit to anything but it. Intellect has a multi-faceted aspect to it that requires one to dedicate time to its long term development and smart can exist with little development and no commitment. Given the choice, many would choose smart over intellect for its worldly appreciation and avoid intellectual pursuit because of its necessary commitment and uncertain value. In this dilemma, pride plays no small role.

How does Pride Contradict Intellect?

Pride is such a beautifully wicked creation that it always takes the form necessary to achieve its goal, which is always to invite anyone and everyone to avoid the work necessary to be our best possible selves. If it were easy to be one's best possible self, more people would accomplish the goal. It is not and more often than not, pride is a significant factor when one falls short. Pride's relationship with intellect is not the exception. Where intellect implores humility as the energy to spur growth, pride has a different agenda. Pride has the ability to sufficiently shape shift and fight on several fronts at the same time. Pride is a masterful illusionist and the smarter one is the more illusions pride has at its disposal.

In the case of intellect, pride has the power to convince one that intellectual pursuit should serve the arbitrary interests of individuals or groups. In this method of operation, the pursuit of intellectual growth is valued only to the extent that it can be quantified and manipulated, often for the accumulation of material gain but not always. In this approach, the intellectual pursuit is not an ever expanding enterprise. It is intentionally directed to meet arbitrary wants. As a consequence, intellectual pursuit has nothing to do with reaching the best possible self. In this approach, the pursuit is simply about the most possible gain. On another front, pride has the ability to effectively suggest to some that intellectual pursuit is not necessary at all.

In this illusion, pride crafts a vision that one's current state of intellectual capacity is sufficient. This illusion is convenient for many simply because it offers a reality where no intellectual work is required at all. In this illusion, it is at least helpful if one is smart. While it can present interestingly, it still lacks any substance. Pride has a way of constructing illusions where intellectual growth is a pursuit of luxury. Indeed, suggesting that there is actually a viable option to learning, growing and getting better. Pride is terribly effective at not only inviting one to settle into complacency but to find in it some joy and reason to stay there. Pride is the inverse of intellect for one important reason; where intellect requires growth, pride invites contentment and satisfaction. The complacency suggested by pride is one where growth is not only an unwelcomed option, it is perceived as an unnecessary want rather than an essential ingredient to achieve any goals we have set for ourselves.

Pride is so effective that in its extreme expression, it will find reasons to mock intellectual pursuit as a frivolous activity engaged by those who have nothing else to do. Pride will find cause to revel in its own ignorance and as often as possible, it will invite others to do so in theirs as well. The seductive appeal of self-righteousness is one of the most compelling forces humans can encounter. Whenever we experience growth, intellectual or otherwise, it is always the outcome of deliberate work and oftentimes inconvenient work.

The Challenge Going Forward

The most important challenge going forward understands what it means to be in pursuit of intellectual growth. The pursuit of intellectual growth is not simply about what books you read or the content within them. The pursuit of intellectual growth is about deliberately and consistently exploring your capacity to not only know and understand but your willingness to expand your capacity. In part, intellectual growth both invites and informs the journey we call life. To the extent that one is not willing to grow intellectually or otherwise, then some part of the self is underfed and malnourished. A condition that can only lead to a kind of death.

A significant challenge to intellectual pursuit is to find routine activities that summon, provoke and welcome serious difficulty about the assumptions we have about the nature of our version of truth. More importantly, we have to welcome challenges to our understandings that indict fundamental values we have about our own identity. Unfortunately, many people are not willing to do so and have already rationalized why it is not a good idea to be forced to recommit, re-evaluate or reassess what we think is important about this life and why we think it so. If we share space with people who are willing to do so, they often awake in us something that we enjoy even if we are frightened of it at the same time. If we refuse to grow tacitly or not, what are we offering to the world, our friends, our children or even our chosen mates?

The pursuit of intellectual growth is connected to all other forms of growth; spiritual, emotional, psychological and otherwise. Interestingly, many people will claim they welcome the work necessary but will do little or nothing to actualize it into their lived experience. Even more interesting, those same people will often times hold others responsible for inadequacies they feel about their lives. There is no duty more primary than the responsibility we have for the absence or presence of growth in our own lives. It is an onus that none of us can delegate to another. Every person, family, community and society has the obligation and shoulders the accountability to work and be better if better is something that is desired.

Chapter X

PRIDE, POLITICS AND SOCIETY

*"Pride's relationship with politics
is covertly dangerous and captivating,
when left unmanaged politics can become
a process by which egos are stroked
and desires fulfilled."*

Pride and Politics

Politics is a fluid concept that means different things in different contexts. In one way or another, it most often refers to the art or science of influencing the behavior and/or perceptions of others. The most frequent and common measurement of success is the achievement of a desired outcome. Can one effectively persuade others to behave in way that meets an arbitrary interest or goal? In some ways, humans have engaged in some sort of political process since humans decided to live in groups with competing interests. When humans have competing needs and interests and it is not possible for everyone to achieve a subjective desired outcome, a political process has to be employed to determine which interests will be addressed. For an individual, that process can be a solitary reflection period to both determine and prioritize needs and wants.

For a family, it could include a discussion where the topic is the feelings and concerns of each member of the family to determine a collective course of action. Groups and nations engage in similar processes to determine collective needs, wants, priorities and actions. In every context, individuals, families and groups, there is a deliberate intent to determine interests and then have those interests addressed. As a matter of consequence, people utilize the resources at their disposal to see their arbitrary matters addressed and/or their wants and needs realized. Rarely is this process in any context absent of the will to leverage one's interests at the expense of another's.

This political reality is only complicated by the introduction of more individuals or groups with even more arbitrary needs and interests. Even in pride's absence, people can and do have very different wants and needs unique to their perception of reality. As such, in the best possible scenarios, there would be some need for an evaluation process that arranges determined interests in a sequence. The established sequence would invariably reflect someone's values and intentions to the benefit of some and the disadvantage of others. Under no circumstance should any political process be understood as a mechanism to identify the greatest possible good because these processes by nature are not designed to achieve that outcome. A political process will determine what needs will be tackled but they should not and cannot purport to determine why any identified need of the process is qualitatively better than another. Pride's role in political processes is relevant because it will often times allow arbitrary wants to be presented as collective needs.

Pride at its base is unexcitingly simple. It often wants to create a sense of value and pleasure through the path of least resistance. Pride will help justify a priority but it does not soul search to determine the value or impact that the pursuit of such a priority has on other important aspects of the whole. To be sure, there are times when the value and impact are more or less important but they are never irrelevant. However, pride would have you believe otherwise. Pride in a political process allows interests to be pursued with surprisingly little concern for the impact of the pursuit. Politics is a process that determines whose interests will be attended to but rarely does it determine why. Pride finds a peculiar residency in politics because of its affection for desire. Every political process has at its essence the desire to have a particular interest undertaken. Pride will take to the interests of desire in any context that it can. When pride finds a role in politics, rarely are needs given the examination they deserve because that often requires commitment and evaluation. Wants rarely require such work and as a consequence, pride seeks to connect to desire because it seeks only to extend pleasurable outcomes with the least amount of effort.

As a consequence, a method commonly used as an incentive to persuade is the fulfillment of a sought after want. Cumbersome needs are rarely, if ever, addressed. Pride's relationship with politics is covertly dangerous and captivating. When left unmanaged, politics can become a process by which egos are stroked and desires fulfilled. When a political process is perverted into a pride serving industry, less and less competing interests are addressed and are substituted by common cravings. The more pride infiltrates a political process, the more danger there is for common cravings to move from an unfortunate side-effect to an unstated goal.

Pride and Society

The ubiquitous presence and the overwhelming impact of pride in society are shockingly under discussed. More importantly, we live in a society where it is not uncommon for a non-profit and religious organizations to be more concerned about their own preservation than serving the communities they have committed themselves to assisting. Many families often times, for justifiable and legitimate reasons, seek the support of assisted living agencies for its aging members. However, frequently, once they are there, many family members can't be bothered for once a week visits. This saddening reality shockingly pales in comparison to some of the behavior of a few people who work in these same facilities. There are doctors who are willing to perform plastic surgery under circumstances that seem to stun anyone with a conscience. There are lawyers who file lawsuits that are little more than comedic materials and they win.

The prideful vanity that seems to be commonplace in the lives of adolescents and young adults seems to be an accepted reality. Certainly, law enforcement officers are frequently faced with circumstances that most other members of society would not subject themselves but that service does not and should not place them above a healthy scrutiny of people who have a near legal monopoly on the use of violence in a democratic society. There are teachers and members of the clergy who do things to and with children that no one charged with the responsibility to protect them should even think about. Pride allows the self to feel fulfilled particularly when the appropriate work has not been done to warrant it. We live in a society where the entire economic structure is predicated on its member's economic consumption. Meaning, two-thirds of the U.S. economy is predicated on consumer consumption while alarming numbers of families and children live below the poverty line.

People are encouraged to buy things they don't need or can't afford and when they can't, they are confronted with not so subtle messages that they don't measure up and sometimes, suggesting they are outright failures. These consumption and prideful messages are so accepted that "Santa only brings the good kids gifts." With surprising regularity, one can hear some refer to their material accumulation as blessings. Certainly, the sentiment is not altogether wrong but it is always convoluted when one connects material gain to "blessings." It is much less common to refer to "blessings" used in circumstances where there is an absence of material gain but an abundance of love, joy, health, friendship and other non-material assets. Leaving the question: Can one live below the poverty line for one's entire existence, having constant need for the basics of human life; food, shelter, love and water and still be considered blessed?

Of course many would say yes but given the choice, many would probably take an empty life filled with material contentment. Pride and society is a topic worthy of more space than will be dedicated in this piece. However, it is important that each of us take this topic seriously and work to address it in the space we occupy in our own hearts and heads but it is vital that we do so with our children and families because they are the cornerstone of any society.

Containing Pride and Releasing Society's Potential

How can pride be contained while releasing society's potential? In all honesty, perhaps there is no single answer to a question as complicated and convoluted as this one. This question probably returns this journey to where it began. The best approach to this maybe is to start with the person in the mirror. How does each of us seek the presence of joy in our lives? In what ways can we utilize the concept humility in our growth and development? To what extent are we appreciating all the goodness in our lives that we know deep in our hearts we don't deserve? How much effort is anyone of us willing to commit to our own development?

Every society has to answer those questions one person at a time. The real question for society is: How does a society reward humility, love and service? It is not entirely irrational for a society to not directly reward these things. Perhaps, those concepts should not be rewarded so as to determine who really believes in them. Society's best defense against pride is family structures that promote the necessary values to manage pride's growth and development. Our commitment to such principles can be measured by our willingness to be inconvenienced by them. When families encourage and nurture its members to be their best possible selves, an entire society is improved.

Containing pride is not an event, it is a commitment. No society can ever completely remove pride because to do so, one would have to remove all the people. In fact, one could make the argument that in some ways, societies need pride to help them find their way. The presence of pride and the resulting battle with it helps societies find ways to support its most vulnerable members. Societies that find ways to respond are societies that survive and societies that don't find healthy ways to respond are forever in danger of dissolving under the weight of their own disillusions, as is true for all individuals, families, groups or nations who leave pride unchecked. In the alternative, in the absence of pride, a society's potential is in effect, limitless when presented with the opportunity to grow from the collective gifts and talents. While learning from individual and collective mistakes remove the ceiling of potential from any society. In effect, providing any given society, group, family or individual with an ever growing opportunity to be the best circumstances will allow, which is all that is ever possible.

A society's most effective tool to contain pride and release the potential of every individual in it is to be ever vigilant about promoting the importance of growth through struggle. It is important that every society perceive threats to their survival simultaneously as opportunities to extend their survival. Sometimes, society's pride can dismiss the grievances of the most vulnerable as trivial and miss an opportunity to make the entire society stronger and healthier. While Pride can sometimes seem to be a society's most natural companion, more often than not, it is a mortal enemy.

CONCLUDING THOUGHTS

While the dangers of pride are significant and many of them identified in this work, pride as do all things, serves a purpose. Much of the human perception of reality is understood through such concepts as duality, balance and opposites. One of the reasons that light has meaning to us is because darkness is part of our awareness. Good in part makes sense to us because there is something we understand to be bad. Are these concepts opposites or examples of balance and duality? That seems to be a determination left for each of us to interpret. Is pride the opposite of humility? Does pride help to provide a framework or balance for concepts such as faith and joy? The pursuit of pride can result in outcomes that one can find favorable but does that make pride a worthy endeavor?

Certainly, if one is driven to accumulate a collection of things that makes one feel worthy of life and living, how bad can that be? Significant matters to be addressed in the lived experience of all humans. In a society that is predicated on competition, vanity and materialism, pride finds a natural space to occupy. In fact, the rejection of pride can have a profound impact on one's material life, spiritual development, psychological framework and emotional state. The positive outcomes that result from prideful industries are often realized at significant costs. It would be dishonest to not acknowledge that there are outcomes of pride that are welcomed and for some, the outcomes are well worth the price. The somewhat sexist and patriarchal saying "What profits a man who gains the world but loses his soul" seems to provide some perspective on this challenge. While it is without question that pride has a place in the human experience, what that place is and how we perceive it seems to be an important issue.

The temptation connected to pride's offerings seem to the author to be awash with more quagmires than most mortals are prepared to handle. Pride's place in the human experience is complicated at best and at worst, it can be perceived as a psychological and spiritual threat that has few equals. It is in many ways prideful to make absolute claims about pride and its effect on the human condition. The primary purpose of this work is to invite the reader to explore the role of pride they perceive in the world. It is the belief of the author that these kinds of explorations can encourage positive development for an individual, family, organization or society. While no result can be guaranteed by the effort, the value offered by the process is an opportunity to identify areas in need of work. Identifying areas in need of work is an essential component to get better at anything, where being better is the goal. This book for some, including the author, attempts to support a life-long struggle for each of us to become whatever it is we wish to become and to leave behind whatever it is we wish to leave behind.

CPSIA information can be obtained
at www.ICGtesting.com
Printed in the USA
BVOW08s0325141117
500280BV00012B/1037/P